SNOOPING CAN BE

Contagious

LINDA HUDSON HOAGLAND

LITTLE CREEK BOOKS
A division of Jan-Carol Publishing, Inc.
Johnson City, TN

LITTLE CREEK BOOKS
A division of Jan-Carol Publishing, Inc.
Johnson City, TN

SNOOPING CAN BE CONTAGIOUS

LINDA HUDSON HOAGLAND

Published March 2013

ISBN: 978-1-939289-13-1
Library of Congress Control Number: 2013934258

You may contact the publisher:
Jan-Carol Publishing, Inc.
PO Box 701
Johnson City, TN 37605
E-mail: publisher@jancarolpublishing.com
www.jancarolpublishing.com

DEAR READER

I am entrusting with you my second volume of the *Lindsay Harris Murder Mystery Series* in which Lindsay discovers how far and how long the bonds of friendship can stretch and endure as she helps Jed Chandler, her friend, try to prove the innocence of Jed's former classmate.

Lindsay is a character partially formed from my years as a legal secretary/assistant and my desires to make the job a little more interesting than the repetitive typing of one legal form after another.

I hope you like Lindsay and her antics as she explores the world that surrounds her to find answers that make sense.

This is the second of a series of mystery stories that will follow Lindsay, her family, and her friends as she tries to outrun all of the trouble and mischief that she blunders into without much effort on her part leading her to the thought that *Snooping Can Be Contagious*.

I have been a long time and proud resident of Southwest Virginia and the Appalachian Mountains in my small Town of Tazewell. I am a retired employee of the Tazewell County Public Schools where I worked as a purchase order clerk for more than twenty years. I have two sons, Mike and Matt, who are wonderful, of course, a daughter-in-law, Becky, and soon-to-be daughter-in-law, Donna.

I am now 64 and I have been writing all of my life but I didn't get my first book published until 2006. I have been trying to make up for lost time since then because I waited so very long to get it done.

I would like to welcome you to my world of Lindsay Harris as she tries to live her life one day at a time through the pages of *Snooping Can Be Contagious*.

Yours truly,

Linda Hudson Hoagland, Author

ACKNOWLEDGMENTS

Janie C. Jessee, my publisher, earns a special mention because she has enough faith in me to think that I might be able to continue writing a mystery series. Thank you, Janie, for allowing me to do what I love to do.

Tammy Robinson Smith, my friend and fellow writer, deserves my thanks for the encouragement and advice I have received.

Thanks to the Appalachian Authors Guild, Lost State Writers Guild, West Virginia Writers and Reminiscent Writers for allowing me to be a member and participate in functions that have allowed me to improve my writing skills.

This book is dedicated to:
MIKE & DONNA
MATT & BECKY
They are my world.

Chapter 1

"Mom, I've got a babysitting job," shouted a jubilant Ellen as she raced into the house slamming doors and nearly tripping over the laundry basket I had strategically placed in her path. It had been my intention that she pick up the laundry basket and take it to her bedroom to be emptied of the clean, folded clothes that belonged to Ellen and her twin sister, Emily.

"Whoa, slow down, Ellen, before you break your neck," I said sternly.

"Did you hear me, Mom? I have a babysitting job," she repeated.

"Yes, I heard you. Where is the job going to be? Who for?" I asked in a soft tone as I tried to get her to calm down.

"Don't worry, Mom, I know the man who wants me to watch his two kids. I think you know him, too. He lives just down the road a piece," Ellen explained.

"Where do you know him from, young lady?" I asked in a half-way angry tone.

"Just around. I've seen him walking with his kids, playing in the park, and at the grocery store when you make me go shopping with you," said Ellen in a whining, pleading voice. It was the same voice that drove me crazy.

"Don't you dare start whining, Ellen. What is his name and how many kids does he have with their ages, please," I asked trying not to scold Ellen.

"Steven Armstrong and his kids are James, age six, and Jackie, age three. I know how to babysit, Mom. We had a class at school and I received an "A". So did Emily and she is going to go with me. We can split the money he pays us," Ellen answered.

"When?" I asked.

"Tomorrow evening. He wants us there at six," Ellen said with excitement.

"How much is he going to pay you?" I asked.

"Five dollars an hour," Ellen said softly.

"The going rate for a certified babysitter is ten dollars an hour, isn't it?" I asked.

"Yes, Mom, but this is our first time so I thought five dollars would be enough," said Ellen in her own defense.

"Where do Steven Armstrong and his kids live?" I asked.

"At the corner of Valley View and Riverside in the big white house," answered Ellen.

"I didn't know anyone was living in that house. When did they move in there?" I asked skeptically.

"I don't know, Mom. He's been around for a long time," said Ellen trying not to whine.

"Is there a Mrs. Armstrong?" I asked.

"Not that I know of," replied Ellen.

"That's not good," I admonished.

"Why?" asked Ellen.

"Well, he might be trying to lure you to his house to do bad things," I said.

"Stop it, Mom. Not every man is a criminal or pervert," snapped Ellen.

"I know, I know, but I meet an awful lot of them at work. Wayne defends all kinds of perverts and whatever, so I see them all of the time. If I don't know them personally, I read about them in the files," I explained in my own defense as a legal secretary.

"Can we, Mom? Can we babysit?" Ellen begged as Emily looked on without saying a word.

"Let me think about it, girls."

"Pretty please, Mom," chimed both of my daughters.

"I said to let me think about it," I said sternly.

"Think? How long?" asked Emily.

"Give me an hour," I answered.

Both girls walked away downhearted. My usual answer when I have to think about it is 'no.'

I really had to think about this. Babysitting for an unmarried man with two kids didn't fit comfortably into my picture of good things to do for my teenage daughters.

I had to give the man credit for, at least, hiring babysitters for his children.

Maybe I was being over-protective, but mothers were supposed to do that, weren't they?

Exactly one hour later, Ellen and Emily stood in front of me seeking an answer.

"Yes, you can babysit. But – I want a phone number or you can take my cell phone with you. I want you to be able to call me if you need me. Okay, girls?" I said in a rush of words so I wouldn't have a chance to change my mind.

"Have you two seen Ryan?" I asked as the thought of the whereabouts of my ten-year- old son popped into my mind.

"He said he was going to be playing with Bobby," answered Ellen who seemed to know everything about everybody as of late.

"He needs to tell ME where he's going," I said sternly.

"He tried but you were on the telephone and Bobby was in a hurry so he told me," explained Ellen.

"Did he say when he was coming home since I wasn't able to give him a time to be here?" I probed.

"Before dinner, Mom. That reminds me, what are we having for dinner?" Emily asked.

"Fish sticks with macaroni and cheese; you all seem to like that combination and it is easy to prepare," I said as I walked towards the kitchen to start cooking.

I knew Ryan had to be lying when he said he couldn't tell me he was going to Bobby's because I was on the phone. The telephone had not rung one time since I arrived from work, nor had I made any phone calls.

Ryan hadn't been the same since his father stole him and took him to Pennsylvania almost a year ago. Justin took all of my kids on a trip to an amusement part and to see their grandparents. Of course, that was a total and complete falsehood.

He had actually stolen the three of them with the intention of keeping them with him forever.

That didn't work out and he brought them back to me, thank God.

That experience had damaged Ryan to the point where he found it necessary to lie to me quite often.

I had let most of the little white lies pass without saying anything about them to Ryan even though he knew that I knew he wasn't telling the whole, complete truth. That was probably a mistake now that I have thought about it a little more.

Ryan was working his way into bigger and better lies to tell me and I didn't want to hear them.

I had worked myself past the problem with Ellen and Emily babysitting. I had accepted my decision so it was time to move on.

I had to work on Ryan's dilemma or should I say my dilemma with Ryan?

Chapter 2

I had the food prepared and piping hot at six o'clock.

The girls were home and waiting to be told to come to the kitchen to fill their plates but Ryan was still nowhere to be seen.

Being a single mother can be so frustrating at times, especially if you have kids that aren't babies anymore, but aren't grown-ups either.

I told the girls to get their food and take it to their room so I could have a talk with Ryan when he finally walked through the door.

My tummy was beginning to rumble but I was determined to wait for Ryan and eat with him at the small table in our kitchen together.

I glanced at the clock and it was almost seven, making Ryan an hour late already.

I left the kitchen in search of my address book to look up the number for Bobby's telephone.

"Mrs. Smith, this is Lindsay Harris. I'm Ryan's mother. May I speak with my son?" I said trying to hide my irritation.

"Mrs. Harris..."

"Lindsay, please call me Lindsay."

"Okay, Lindsay. Ryan isn't here. I haven't seen him all evening. I was going to call you because Bobby told me he would be at Ryan's house," she said as her voice filled with concern.

"Do you have any idea where they might be?" I asked.

"No, I was hoping you would know," she answered.

"I'm going to hang up and start making some phone calls to Ryan's other friends. I suggest you do the same. Please call me if you find out where they are and I will do the same for you. Okay?" I said in a controlled tone. I could feel tears of fear, anger, and frustration building up behind my eyes.

I heard Mrs. Smith's phone click off so I pressed my button to do the same.

"Ellen, Emily, come here!" I shouted as I grabbed my address book again.

The girls weren't moving fast enough to suit me so I yelled again.

"Ellen, Emily, in here right now!"

I hear the slapping of bare feet against the hardwood floor of the hallway.

"What, Mom?" shouted Ellen breathlessly as she came to a halt in front of me.

"Ryan isn't home yet. Do you know where he and Bobby were going? Don't tell me it was to Bobby's house because he isn't there and neither is Bobby," I said angrily.

"He said he was going to Bobby's," sputtered Emily.

"He didn't say anything else?" I demanded.

"No, no, he didn't. I would tell you if he did," said Emily as she fought back angry tears.

"I know, Emily. I'm sorry. I'm just worried," I said to console her the best that I could.

I looked at Ellen.

"Did he say anything to you, Ellen?"

She didn't answer me.

"Ellen?"

"No, he didn't say anything but I saw him and Bobby meet up with another boy," said Ellen as she gazed at her feet.

"What boy?" I snapped.

"I don't know him. I never saw him before," she said.

"What did he look like?" I asked.

"I don't know," whined Ellen.

"It's important, Ellen. Try and remember, please," I pleaded.

"He was about a head taller than Ryan," said Ellen.

"That's good, Honey. Now, what color was his hair?" I urged.

"Brown, I think," she answered.

"What was he wearing?" I continued.

"Jeans and a tee shirt. Just like Ryan. I don't remember anything else," Ellen said.

"Emily, do you know anyone like that?" I said as I stared at her.

"No, I didn't see him," Emily replied.

"Emily, I want you to go outside, go to the left, walk up the street knocking on the doors of our neighbors for a couple of blocks, and ask if anyone has seen Ryan," I instructed.

"Okay," said Emily without the usual 'I don't want to do that' glare.

"Ellen, you turn right and do the same thing," I said.

"Aw, Mom, that's so embarrassing," whined Ellen.

"Do as I say, Ellen, and stop whining," I said sternly.

Ellen frowned and stomped out the door following her sister.

I started dialing phone numbers as my mind raced from one tragic possibility to another. I had talked to more than twenty people when I reached the end of the phone numbers with negative results.

Moments later Ellen and Emily walked through the door shaking their heads from side to side.

"Now, what?" I asked my girls.

I heard the back door off of the kitchen squeak on its hinges.

7

"Is that you, Ryan?" I screamed as I jumped up from the chair I was sitting in positioned next to the telephone that I had spent an hour dialing.

"Yes, it's me," Ryan screamed back at me.

That screaming response ran all over my frayed nerves.

"Get in here now, boy!" I said loudly as I tried desperately to control my temper.

He stood in front of me.

I looked him over from head to toe before speaking again.

"Where were you, Ryan?" I asked.

"With Bobby. I'm sorry I'm late, Mom," he said as he looked at his feet.

"Not good enough, Ryan. Where were you and Bobby?" I asked.

"At Bobby's," he said as he continued to look down.

"No, Ryan, you were not at Bobby's house," I said sternly.

"We went to Billy's house," he said softly.

"Who is Billy?" I demanded.

"He is a new kid, Mom. He just moved into the Jameson house. You know the people who live on the next street over behind us. We just have to walk though the trees in the back to get there," he explained.

"Did Bobby go home?" I asked. I knew I would have to call Bobby's mother if he didn't.

"Yeah, he did. He left for home when I did."

"What were you doing?" I asked.

"Nothing," he stammered.

"All of those hours at Billy's house and you did nothing? Stop lying to me, Ryan," I said in an obviously controlled tone.

"We were just hanging out at Billy's. That's all, Mom," he said.

8

"Go get your dinner, Ryan, and sit down at the kitchen table to eat it. I'll be there in a minute to join you," I instructed my almost penitent son.

"Em, El, thank you for helping me. I love you both. Now, go on to your room, okay?" I said as I tried to smile at my girls.

Both girls gladly raced from the room to escape the tension.

Ryan was filling his plate when I entered the kitchen. He turned to leave the kitchen.

"No, Ryan, I want you to sit down here at the table and eat with me," I told him.

"Yes, ma'am."

I filled my plate with the cold food and placed it on the table. I took a bite of a fish stick and grimaced. I don't like cold fish sticks. I rose from the table and placed my plate in the microwave. After heating up the fish and macaroni, I sat down again.

Ryan had already devoured his food.

This was going to be a test of wills.

I ate my food slowly. I wanted him to wait for me this time.

Ryan fidgeted in his seat, inspected his fingernails, and looked at everything in the room except me.

I ate my last morsel of food and rose to place my plate into the sink.

Ryan stood up to leave.

"Sit down, Ryan," I commanded.

He lowered his behind back into the chair.

"You know when we are supposed to eat dinner, don't you, Ryan?"

"Yes, ma'am."

"You know you are supposed to tell me where you go at any time, right?"

"Yes, ma'am."

"You know you should be dealt some kind of punishment. Isn't that right, Ryan?"

9

"Yes, ma'am."

"Well, I'm too angry to deal with the punishment now, Ryan," I said between clinched teeth.

"Yes, ma'am," he sighed.

"Go to your room."

"Yes, ma'am."

I washed the dishes so I could allow myself to unwind from the fears of losing my son to God knows what tragic event.

Bedtime couldn't come soon enough. My mind was tired.

Chapter 3

The next morning I roused each of my brood for school. The girls were finishing up middle school and Ryan had just entered his first year at the same school. All three of them in the same school made it convenient because they all rode the same school bus.

I was sure Ryan wanted to ask me about his promised punishment but I wouldn't let him. I wasn't ready to dish it out, not yet. I had discovered the fact that the longer I waited, the more he worried about it. I found that the worry part of it was better than the actual corporal punishment or grounding him to the house with no television or telephone.

After the kids were on their way, I jumped into the car and headed for work where I was a legal assistant/secretary for Wayne Maxwell, Attorney at Law.

Working for Wayne Maxwell was far from being the best job in the world but it was the only one I could find at the time.

I had moved my family, consisting of my twin daughters, Ellen and Emily, along with Ryan, my son, from the small town in Ohio where I could see them all destined for no good. It seemed that all of the juvenile boys, friends of Ryan's, were being routed one at a time to the reformatory and the juvenile girls were following suit. I didn't want that to happen to my son and daughters. I wanted only the best for them and that didn't include staying in Ohio.

When we arrived in Virginia, I had no job, nothing that could sustain me and my children for any time except a small bit of savings that was dwindling rapidly.

I applied for a job in Wayne Maxwell's law office and it was offered to me at minimum wage. I took the job in order to get myself established in the area. I have been looking for a new, different job ever since the first day I walked into Wayne's newly constructed law office on Church Street just off of Main. Wayne had increased my wages just enough to keep me under his thumb.

When I arrived at the office the front door was unlocked and the lights in the front office were blazing. Anna must have already arrived, I thought as I entered the building.

"Lindsay, is that you?" shouted a familiar voice from the end of the hallway.

I was wrong. Anna must not be here; it was Wayne that was calling me.

"Yes, sir," I said as I winced as if punched in the gut.

"Come back here. I need you to do something right away," he continued to shout.

On my way down the hallway, I threw my handbag and tote containing my lunch onto my desk. This was not the way to start a good day.

"Wayne, what do you need?" I asked as I entered his office.

"How far along are you on the Jones closing?" he demanded.

"Not very. You haven't done the title search and I need that to type the deed and deed of trust," I explained.

"I did that yesterday. It's in my dictation," he said.

"You didn't give me a tape yesterday," I said knowing this was going to lead to an argument if I let it.

"I left it on your desk when I went to lunch," he said.

"I didn't see it, Wayne, and I was here all day. I never left the building," I said.

"I know I left it on your desk yesterday afternoon," he snapped.

I forced myself to walk to his credenza where his dictating machine was located where I pressed the eject button and up popped a tape that had been used up almost to the end.

"This tape, Wayne?" I asked as I tried to hide my smirk.

"I don't know how it got back into my machine. I know I placed it on your desk. Did you put it back in there?" he demanded.

I removed the tape from the machine and shook my head.

"This is the first time I've seen it. I'll get started on it right away," I said as I grabbed the folder that had JONES in capital letters written on the tab.

I knew better than to wait for an apology. God would strike me dead before that happened.

Before I settled into the preparation of the deed and deed of trust, I wanted to find Anna. She was usually here before I arrived and I saw no sign of her when I came through her office upon entering the building.

"Jeez, I keep losing people," I mumbled as my mind went back to Ryan's absence the previous evening.

No Anna anywhere, so I went into the kitchen to make coffee for all of us.

The telephone started ringing and I knew Wayne would not answer it. I raced into Anna's office and punched the button for Line 1.

"Wayne Maxwell's law office, may I help you?" I said as I struggled to gain control of my breathing.

"Lindsay?" said a weak voice.

"Yes?"

"This is Anna. I think I have caught some kind of virus. I don't feel well at all," she whispered so low that I could barely hear her.

"Boy, Anna, you sound sick. Stay home and get over this," I said compassionately.

I transferred the telephone lines to my extension in my office.

"This day is not getting any better," I mumbled.

I prepared all of the necessary forms for the Jones closing in between the constant interruptions of phone calls, lobby walk-ins, and frequent shouts from Wayne to come to his office.

I was determined to go home with a good mood. I had a natural tendency to take my frustration out on my family members as I had to make an obvious effort not to treat them badly no matter what.

I arrived home at 5:30 PM and my children met me at the door when I entered the house. It was Friday evening and we usually do something together as a family.

This was the anxiously awaited evening for a trip to the local movie theater where we planned to watch *The Hunger Games*.

"Okay, guys, it's not time for the movie yet. Let me change clothes and we can go to McDonald's before the movie," I said as I made my way back to my bedroom.

It was going to be a jeans and tee shirt night and I was going to be a kid just like them.

Chapter 4

Saturday morning arrived too early for my taste. I had stayed up too late Friday night after consuming popcorn, soda pop, and candy at the movie theater. We all enjoyed the movie and late night fun of playing Monopoly along with eating and drinking more junk food.

My punishment had not materialized for Ryan; meaning that I had done nothing except let him worry. It seemed to have done the trick, at least temporarily, because he was doing as I asked without an argument; not even rolling his eyes.

It was the day of the babysitting job for my girls and they were both excited.

The first thing on the agenda for Emily and Ellen was to introduce me to the gentleman who had hired them to babysit. I also wanted to meet the two children for whom my girls would be caring. After the introduction I would obtain the telephone number and give him my number in case there was any kind of problem.

I don't think I would have followed the same protocol if a woman had done the hiring, but a single man and teenage girls planted a red flag in my mind.

"Come on, Emily, Ellen, I don't want to get started on any-thing else until I meet the man you are working for," I told my daughters as I tried to hurry them along with their tasks so I could get them out of the house and into the car.

"Ryan, do you want to go with us?" I asked my son.

"Can I stay here, Mom?" he asked.

"Yes, no trouble, okay?" I said.

"Mom, please," said Ryan.

"We won't be gone long, Ryan," I told him. Again, I was trying to trust my son.

As luck would have it before I was able to get out of the door and on my way with the girls, the telephone rang.

"Mom, it's Justin," shouted Ryan.

"Jeez," I said softly. I was trying very hard not to say something ugly.

"Girls, go wait for me in the car," I shouted out the front door. "I'll be there in just a minute."

I took the telephone from Ryan,

"Why is he calling me Justin?" demanded my ex-husband and father of my children.

"I don't know. That's the first time I heard him refer to you as Justin and not dad," I answered defensively. It was the normal beginning of a conversation with Justin for me to immediately begin defending myself for committing a wrong I about which I knew nothing.

"I don't like it, Lindsay," he said sternly.

"I'll talk to him, Justin. Now, what do you want?" I asked.

"Actually, I was thinking about picking up the kids and taking them for a picnic," he said.

"Why?" I asked.

"They are my kids, that's why," he snapped.

"They have been your offspring for a few years, you know. Maybe I should have phrased my question as 'Why now?'" I said trying to suppress the sarcasm.

"Marilyn and I have free time. We thought we would spend it with my kids," he explained in a controlled tone. I had heard the name from a previous confrontation with Justin when he stole my children and took them out of state to live forever according to him.

"When did you and Marilyn get married?" I probed.

"We didn't. Marilyn and I aren't married, but we've been together for a few years," he said.

"Oh," I said, "she's just a live-in."

My tongue was tending to be filled with acid and I was having trouble reining in my feelings.

"Lindsay, I don't care what you think about the way I'm living. I want to see my kids and I have a right to see them," he said.

"You have a right to see them, to act like their father, but you must do it at my house under my supervision. That's what the judge said the last time you dragged me into court."

"A picnic? You won't let me take them on a picnic?" he stammered.

"No!" I said loudly. "I don't think you and Marilyn would like to take me along with you. It might be a little crowded."

"Can I, at least, take Ryan fishing?" he continued.

"No," I repeated.

"We'll see about that," he said as he noisily hung up on me.

"Good," I whispered as I glanced at the receiver in my hand. I walked out the door to my car to join my daughters who were waiting patiently.

The drive took only a couple of minutes but I was still upset when we finally arrived at our destination after I had spent several minutes on the phone with Justin.

Talking with Justin made me both angry and sad. I got angry when he even mentioned taking my kids anywhere without me because I knew he wouldn't bring them back to me. I was sad thinking about what we did to each other that was so bad that it led us to this point in life.

I knew I had to shake off the bad feelings I had toward Justin so as not to direct them to Steven Armstrong, the man for whom my daughters would be working.

"Let's go, Mom," shouted Ellen as she jumped out of the car.

Chapter 5

I knocked at Steven Armstrong's front door almost dreading the meeting. I didn't want to think of what I might have to do if Armstrong didn't pass my inspection. I also didn't want to think about the disappointment I would have to heap upon my daughters if I said 'no.'

Armstrong seemed to take a long time to answer the door so I stood patiently waiting while the girls hopped around like they were dancing on hot coals.

Finally, the door opened and Steven Armstrong peered out at us while two small children, one on each side, held firmly to his legs.

"Mr. Armstrong, I'm Lindsay Harris, the mother of Emily and Ellen who say they are going to babysit for James and Jackie tonight. I wanted to meet you and get your telephone number in case there is an emergency," I explained as politely as possible.

Armstrong extended his hand to me after he removed it from the top of James's head. I reached to him and shook his hand firmly. I didn't like a cold fish handshake and I was sure he wouldn't like that in return.

"Come inside," he said when he released my hand. "I'll get that phone number for you."

As he walked off in search of paper and pen, James and Jackie scurried along behind him like little scared rabbits.

I glanced around the house and saw a well-worn rental where kids had taken up residence. I knew for a fact when you had children as young as six and three it was impossible to keep all life signs of habitation out of the living room.

I saw a small rag doll stuffed between the back of a side chair and the seat cushion. Over in the corner of the room were two small trucks parked in front of the wall.

Next to the side chair was a stash of newspapers with the classified section displayed.

I started to walk to the chair so I could see what part of the classified section was showing, but Armstrong returned to the room before I could do so. I wanted to know whether he was looking for a job or looking for a different place to live.

"Here's the phone number," he said handing me a small piece of paper with his name and seven digits scrawled across it. "Is there anything else?"

"Yes, sir. How long will the girls be here with your children?"

"Maybe four hours. No later than ten o'clock. Earlier, I hope," he said nervously. "I'll see that they get home safely. They told me where you live and I'll be happy to walk them or drive them home."

I could see his nervousness and his irritation with my questions. Of course, I would probably be irritated, too, with all of the seemingly stupid questions.

"May I ask what you will be doing? I don't want you driving my girls if you've been drinking," I said sternly.

"Oh, no, Ma'am, I will be at a job interview. I will not be drinking."

"All right, Mr. Armstrong, I will see that the girls get here at six. Thank you for your help and understanding," I said as I walked out of his house with Emily and Ellen trailing behind me.

I was uneasy about my conversation with Mr. Armstrong because he seemed so nervous with me and my questions. Of course, I was uneasy with my decision to let the girls babysit but I knew I was going to have the same doubts with future babysitting jobs.

Fortunately, Emily and Ellen loved small children so it was not going to be a difficult task for them–only me.

Chapter 6

Saturday evening couldn't have been better. The babysitter job only lasted about two hours and the girls were home at 8:15 with cash in hand.

Ryan spent the whole evening in his room. Doing what? I didn't have a clue.

Each time I checked on him he was sprawled on the bed with ear buds attached to his I pod. I didn't know he had become such a music buff.

When I had my children all tucked away in their beds for the night, I pulled out a movie I had wanted to watch and promptly fell asleep before half of it had played. Oh, well, such is life of a single mother.

We had planned as a family to have a lazy, stay at home Sunday.

That was how it started because I actually stayed in bed until eight o'clock which was late for me. I was usually up at five trying to get household chores finished that had remained undone from the prior evening.

Whether I was a married or a single woman, the chores were still there. My children did help but they, too, had responsibilities that sucked up time.

I started a load of the never-ending laundry. Next, was the breakfast preparation and, because it was Sunday, it had to be better than the week day fare of cold cereal and toast.

Bacon, sausage, and fried potatoes were in separate skillets on the electric range in the small kitchen that didn't allow too many people to be tackling breakfast duties.

When I had everything cooked and ready except the eggs, I called my kids to breakfast with a shout outside each closed door.

Emily and Ellen were awake and needed no prompting but Ryan continued to snooze.

"Ryan, time to get up," I shouted as I opened his bedroom door.

He raised his sleepy head and said, "I want to sleep, Mom."

"It's nine o'clock and you need to get out of bed so you can eat breakfast. You can take a nap later if you're still tired and sleepy," I said as I urged him up with my words.

"No, I want to sleep," he mumbled in reply.

"Okay, but I will call you again in an hour. You are not spending your whole morning in bed," I said much more sternly.

I closed his door and let him sleep thinking probably that he had been up late playing his computer games that he loved.

The girls and I had a leisurely breakfast as I tried to coax them into telling me all about their weekly escapades.

Ellen and Emily were active participants in school activities that were mostly academic or service oriented. Neither of my daughters ever wanted to be a cheerleader and I was glad about that even though that could change when they got to high school.

Ryan hadn't decided to participate in any of the extra-curricular activities choosing to play his computer games and hanging out with other boys with the same computer interests.

"Mom, can we go to Amy's house today?" asked Emily cheerfully.

"And do what?" I asked with a smile. I knew the question was coming. I just didn't know which girlfriend would get the nod.

"Just hang," responded Ellen, "nothing in particular."

"How much of that nothing in particular is boy talk?" I asked as I tried to suppress a giggle. My girls were growing up so very quickly.

"Aw, Mom, we don't do that," said Emily as a flush crept up her face.

"Yeah, we do, Em, but, at least, we are nice about it. We really don't try to put anybody down or make fun of them," said Ellen as she, too, was coloring with embarrassment.

"I'm glad, Ellen. Remember, you are not perfect either so there is no need to point out anyone's flaws," I said as my pride ran through me like an adrenaline rush.

"Well, Mom? Can we go?" asked Ellen and Emily in unison which is a twin thing, I guess.

"Yes, you can go but don't wear out your welcome, okay?" I said.

The girls ran from the room to shower and get dressed in jeans and tee-shirts which was their official teenage daily wear.

It was eleven o'clock and Ryan had yet to enter the world of the wide awake. I had actually let him sleep two extra hours not the one I had threatened.

"Ryan, get up, now!" I shouted from outside his bedroom door.

"I'm awake, Mom. I'll be out in a little while," he shouted from the other side of the door.

"Do you want some eggs?" I asked loudly.

"No, I'm not hungry," he replied in a surly tone.

I walked into the kitchen shaking my head acknowledging the fact that my baby boy was also growing up. I was going to have to figure out what I can do to make Ryan the same boy he used to be before his father stole him and took him to Pennsylvania to become a permanent member of his family removing me from his life forever.

I left him alone and he finally came out of the room in the middle of the afternoon. I had set aside a plate with bacon and sausage on it that he attacked with glee.

Ryan's mood had changed from surly to smiling and laughter. For whatever reason, I was happy to see the change. Ryan and I were engrossed in a scary movie when both of my daughters burst through the door screaming to me to change the television channel.

I switched to the local news and heard the newsman telling the viewing area about a double homicide that took place in the middle of the Clinch River.

Witnesses have stated that Steven Armstrong rowed a boat to the center of the Clinch River with his two small children ostensibly to teach them how to fish. The center is reportedly the deepest part of the river. Later, when Armstrong returned the boat rental, he was alone, no children in sight. There is an investigation under way to locate the two children, James, age 6, and Jackie, age 3.

We will report updates as we receive them.

"Mom, those are the kids we babysat for, remember?" said an excited Emily.

"Yes, I sure do. I knew there was something wrong with that guy. I felt it in my bones," I said as I remembered my internal conflict over the babysitting job.

"Mom," said Ellen, "those were really cute kids and they were nice, too. We didn't have to threaten them in any way. They just sat there and played the whole time he was gone. I guess we were lucky that nothing bad happened while we were there."

"You've got that right," agreed Emily.

"Maybe we are wrong. Maybe he didn't drown his kids. Was there a witness to the drowning?" I asked as I tried to understand the story.

"Not that I know of. They haven't reported it on the news," said Emily as she, too, pondered the reason for killing your children, especially children that were so very young.

"Mom, maybe he didn't kill them" said Ellen. "Nobody saw him do that. Maybe they were wrong."

"I certainly hope so, Ellen," I said as I tried to steer the conversation to better trains of thought.

"Do you have any homework, girls?" I said as they left the room and entered the kitchen.

"No, Mom, we already did it," said Ellen as I heard the refrigerator door slam.

"Don't snack, girls. I'm starting dinner right now," I said as I left the remote in Ryan's hand so he could continue to watch his scary movie.

"What are we having, Mom?" asked Emily.

"Fried chicken with the fixings," I answered cheerfully.

"Kentucky Fried?" asked Ellen,

"No, Lindsay fried," I replied with a giggle.

I was sorry to see my weekend come to an end. I truly enjoyed my family time with my kids and I dreaded every Monday because it brought with it Wayne Maxwell, Attorney at Law.

Chapter 7

I wondered what mood of Wayne's I would have to placate this morning. His mood swings were such that I wondered if he were manic depressive or bipolar. Perhaps he would spin himself into a normal, lawyerly existence, I hoped.

"Girls, get a move on! The bus will be here soon. The same goes for you, Ryan," I shouted at my brood.

Ryan walked out the front door first where he sullenly waited for the arrival of the bus. The girls left next chattering away about what, I didn't have a clue.

I ran to my car, climbed in and prayed, "Dear God, let Wayne be a reasonable, sane man today just like Everett who doesn't have an evil bone in his body. Amen."

Everett was about 20 years older than Wayne but the years had treated Everett well, at least, it seemed that way. He was very even tempered and showed no displays of uncontrollable emotions other than laughter. He liked to do that a lot, laugh I mean.

Everett and Wayne were polar opposites, especially when Wayne was in a mood.

The lights were burning brightly inside the office so I hoped Anna, the receptionist, was the one who had flipped all of the switches.

I turned the door knob slowly and entered the lobby as quietly as I could just in case Anna wasn't the one who lit the lights.

"Hey, Lindsay," said a cheerful young lady who looked to be fresh out of high school which was exactly what Anna was.

"I'm so glad you are here, Anna. Are you feeling better?"

"Yes, I began to feel like a human over the weekend. I hope I didn't cause you too much trouble with my being sick."

"No–no–it was better that you stay home than to make us all sick. I just missed your smiling face," I said.

As soon as I finished speaking, the telephone rang and our nice comfortable feeling melted away.

"Wayne Maxwell, Attorney at Law," chirped Anna…"I'm sorry he isn't here yet, Judge Mullins. May I take a message and have him call you as soon as he arrives?"…"Yes, sir, I will let him know. Bye, Judge Mullins."

"What was that about?" I asked Anna.

"Judge Mullins wants Wayne to handle the defense of the man who murdered his two children," she said excitedly.

"You're kidding?" I asked.

"Do you know anything about it?" Anna asked me.

"Not really. Is this a pro bono case? Judge Mullins wouldn't be calling unless it was for the public defense fund."

"He didn't say, but I think I see Wayne pulling into the parking lot," said Anna as her smile disappeared.

"I'd better get back to my office before he gets in here," I whispered to Anna as I walked downed the hall.

I heard Wayne enter the office with his usual slamming and banging to announce his arrival. The noise came to a halt when Anna gave him his phone messages with the one from Judge Mullins on the top.

As soon as I separated the pile of papers I had on my desk placing them into workable stacks, I heard my name shouted loudly.

"Lindsay, come in here," he screamed. I don't think the idea of using the intercom ever occurred to him.

I rose from my chair, grabbing a pen and pad as I walked briskly to his office.

"Yes, sir," I said as I walked through the doorway.

Chapter 8

"Lindsay, sit down." commanded Wayne.

"Is there something wrong?" I asked as I displayed concern.

"Well, no. I don't know. Maybe," he sputtered.

I was amazed to see him at a loss for words. I didn't think that was possible.

"What is it, Wayne? Can I help?" I said as I watched his face closely.

"Yes, you can. I will probably need a lot of help from you; maybe a lot of late hours in fact," he said calmly.

"Okay, Wayne, what is it?" I pleaded.

"Judge Mullins has asked me to handle the Armstrong case. It is basically pro bono but the Public Defense Fund will pay for most of my out of pocket expenses. I'm going to have to take it. I really don't have a choice," he explained.

"Why don't you have a choice?" I asked so he would have to tell me.

"If you must know, Lindsay, you don't say 'no' to the judge. It can cost us in the future. Also, I think it will be good publicity for me," he said in an almost sarcastic tone.

"I'll do whatever you want me to do, Wayne. You know that," I said in encouragement.

"Good, good, that's what I needed to hear from you. The arraignment hearing is the first thing after lunch. That's all I have to do appearance-wise for now. I will gather copies of all of the paperwork that has been filed as soon as the court knows that I will be representing Armstrong. Next, I will have to file a Discovery Motion to gather the information that hasn't been filed for public record," he said as he returned to his Wayne business-like tone.

"Yes, sir," I replied.

"What are you working on right now?" he asked.

"The Jones closing because they want it completed as soon as possible. It's scheduled for day after tomorrow. I'm entering and printing all of the paperwork today. It's on your calendar for 4:00 o'clock on Wednesday," I answered.

"What else?" he asked.

"The Saracin closing, but you haven't done the title search so I haven't tried to schedule it yet. The same goes for the Edwards closing," I answered.

"I will try to get both of those searches finished this morning before I go to the arraignment," he said as he shook his head to emphasize his effort.

"Yes, sir," I said in agreement.

"In the meantime, you need to get as much of the work finished as you possibly can on all three closings and make me a file for Steven Armstrong."

"Yes, sir," was all I could get out before he dismissed me by turning his back to me.

I walked from his office directly to Anna's office.

"Does Wayne have any appointments today?" I asked hoping the answer was 'no'.

"I don't have anything for him," she replied after glancing at her desk calendar.

"I don't either, thank God," I said. "He is going to be at the courthouse most of the day and I don't have to reschedule anything. It's going to get really busy around here, Anna. You will probably need to fasten your seat belt because it will probably be a bumpy ride."

"I'm ready," she responded with a panicky look on her pretty face.

"It'll be okay, Anna, I promise you. The only ones that will feel the heavy pressure are Wayne and me. You will get the edges of it," I said as I tried to help her eliminate the panic. "I won't let him pile the pain onto your shoulders, I promise."

Anna finally smiled but the smile was only a flicker.

Chapter 9

With Wayne out of the office for most of the day, my progress on the pile of real estate closings was good. All paperwork was completed for the Jones closing and everything that could be done without the title search information was completed on the Saracin and Edwards closings. I felt good with what I had accomplished and Anna was beginning to feel a little better about the up and coming barrage of work to be done.

"Lindsay, there is a Jed Chandler on Line 1," said Anna softly because she thought the call was of a personal nature.

"Thanks, Anna," I said as I punched the button.

"Hey, Jed, what can I do for you?" I said cheerfully.

"Talk to me. Tell me what's going on in your life," he said in a loud voice as he fought to speak over the sound of traffic because he was driving his car.

"The kids are doing great, I'm fine, and all is right with the world," I responded in a tired but cheerful tone.

"I heard that your boss is handling the defense on the double murder case?" he said in a quieter tone as if he didn't want anyone else to hear him.

"Yes, but I haven't seen anything on it yet. All I have done is make up a blank file folder," I answered quietly.

"We need to get together and talk, Lindsay," he said. "It's real important. You probably need to get your friend, Marnie, involved in this."

"Sure, come over this evening and I'll give Marnie a call and ask her to come, too."

As soon as I hung up from Jed's conversation, I dialed Marnie's office number. She worked as a file clerk for the Commonwealth Attorney whose job it was to prosecute the people Wayne defended.

"Hey, Marn," I said when she answered my call.

"Hi, Linds, what do you need?" she said in a loud whisper.

"Boss close by?" I asked.

"Yes, sure, no problem," she answered in her cryptic conversational tone.

"Can you come by the house at six this evening? Jed will be there and he wants to talk to both of us," I said in a rush of words.

"Six, yes, fine, see you then," she said and hung up on me.

"Oh well. I'll talk to her later," I mumbled as I returned the receiver to its rest.

Anna came through my office doorway with gossip on her mind.

"Who is Jed Chandler? New fella?"

"No. Yes. I mean, he is the guy who took Joe Bristol's place at the newspaper. Joe asked me to help him so I am," I answered.

"Do you like him?" asked Anna.

"He is more my age, if that is what you're asking. I'm really going to miss Joe. He was like my second son. He said he would keep in touch and let me know how the wife and baby are doing," I said with a smile.

At five o'clock I was preparing to go home to start my second shift; this time I would be working for my family. Before I could get the door locked, Wayne was standing in front of me.

"Lindsay, I need to talk to you before I leave," he said sternly.

"Sorry, Wayne," I said sheepishly, "I have people coming to the house at six. I need to get home and feed my kids before they get there."

His frown of disapproval appeared on his angry, red face.

"I told you I would need you to stay late," he said sternly.

"Yes, sir, but I had no idea you meant today. I just opened a file and put it on your desk along with the file for the Jones closing."

"All right, all right, but I will need you to stay late maybe tomorrow. In the meantime I will dictate instructions onto a tape. You can do it tomorrow," he said in a huff.

"Yes, sir," I said as I rushed out the door.

On the way home I picked up two pizzas to feed the kids and friends. I reached my front door with food in hand when Marnie pulled into my driveway followed by Jed which was a total surprise. Jed was usually late to everything.

"Come on, you guys. I've got the food so we can all eat."

Chapter 10

The pizza was devoured by all and my children departed for their rooms to work on homework.

"Jed, what's so important?" I asked when the three of us were alone.

"I'll get to that but I need to ask you and Marnie if you know anything about the Armstrong case?" he said conspiratorially.

I waited for Marnie to speak first in answer.

Marnie looked from me to Jed and said, "No, I usually don't see anything until they are ready to put the prepared file into the cabinets and most likely when it is completed or delayed for whatever reason. So – I can truthfully say I don't know anything about it."

"The only thing I have done is to prepare a file folder for Wayne. I haven't seen anything legal. I can tell you that I have met Steven Armstrong and his two children, James and Jackie," I said with a smirk.

"You have actually met him?" questioned Jed.

"Yes and my girls babysat for his children," I said in explanation.

"Do you think he drowned his kids?" asked Jed point blank.

"I don't know him well enough to form an opinion," I sputtered in response.

"You certainly could hazard a guess," coaxed Jed.

"Let me think about it, Jed," I said.

"How about you, Marnie? Have heard any rumors? Maybe you've met him? Do you think he did it?" Jed asked.

"I've heard there are witnesses," Marnie said.

"To what? What did they see?" Jed urged.

"He rowed out to the middle of the river with his children. They saw him do that," said Marnie.

"Did they see him drown his children?" Jed asked.

"No, they didn't," said Marnie.

"Okay, now that you've had time to think, Linds, what do you believe?"

"I want to know why you are giving Marnie and me the third degree about this, Jed. Are you writing an article for the newspaper? If you are, I can't tell you anything," I said harshly.

"You and Marnie seem to know things that happen around here before anyone else. Why is that, Lindsay?" he snapped.

"Luck, Jed, my girls introduced me to Armstrong so I would know for whom they were babysitting. I doubt I would have ever met him if that hadn't happened," I said in explanation. "Why all the interest in Armstrong?"

"We went to school together," answered Jed softly. "Never in a million years would I believe that he would kill his own children."

"What do you think happened, Jed," I asked with concern.

"I don't know," he answered softly.

"What are you going to do?" I asked Jed as I studied his face.

"Well, your little hobby of sticking your nose in where it doesn't belong has rubbed off onto me. Now you know that snooping can be contagious," he said with a broad smile.

"I don't snoop," I said defending myself with a giggle.

"Yes, you do," said a laughing Marnie. "You always seem to drag me into your ploys to uncover the truth as you think it should be told."

"It's not me instigating the search for the truth this time, not that I wouldn't have done it eventually, Marnie. My girls babysat for his children. He was actually alone with my girls. Anything could have happened," I said sadly.

"What can we do, Jed?" Marnie asked.

"Keep your ear to the ground and let me know what's happening," instructed Jed. "That goes for both of you."

"This isn't going to end up in the newspaper, it is?" I asked.

"No, Linds, this is personal with no newspaper involved; not from me, that is."

"In that case, I will tell you what I really think. I don't believe he could drown James and Jackie. I believe he was and is a very depressed man, but he wouldn't or couldn't kill his babies. My Emily and Ellen trusted him enough to babysit for his kids for him. I guess I should trust their instincts on this," I said earnestly.

"Good...good...Lindsay. I'm going to dig up anything on him that I can find in the newspaper or public records. That should get me started on his background."

"Okay, now that the serious discussion is over, what's new with you, Jed?"

"Not much, just the same old same old," he said with a shrug.

Chapter 11

Jed and Marnie left for their individual homes while I cleaned up after everyone so I could get ready for bed.

While I was finishing the dishes the phone rang. I started to dry my hands of dish water when I realized the phone wasn't ringing anymore.

I walked to the kitchen extension and picked up the receiver as quietly as I could. I held it to my ear and heard my ex-husband talking to our son, Ryan.

"...don't tell your mom. It's a secret, okay, Ryan?" said Justin in a whisper.

"No, Dad, I won't tell. Bye," answered Ryan followed by the sound of the receiver being dropped onto its cradle.

I hung up my receiver where I had been eavesdropping and walked rapidly to stand outside of Ryan's bedroom door. I reached my hand up to knock but thought better of it. Tomorrow morning would be good enough for my interrogation. That's what it would be, an interrogation. I truly wanted to know the secret and I expected my son to tell me all about it.

I had learned years earlier to never trust Justin. He would tell me one thing and then do the exact opposite. I really couldn't abide a liar; especially one who did it all the time.

I returned to the kitchen to finish the dishes and extinguish the lights. I was tired physically, but exhausted mentally. That's how I got when Justin re-entered my life for any reason.

I knew the conversation between Ryan and his father was going to weigh heavily on my mind. I lay down on my bed hoping I would sleep because I really needed the rest in order to deal with Wayne. My eyes closed but my brain was continuing to spin.

The back door opened with a creaking sound. A dark figure entered the kitchen and found his way to Ryan's bedroom. The dark figure opened the bedroom door and entered to see an anxiously waiting Ryan. The dark figure scooped Ryan up in his arms as if he weighed nothing and carried him through the doorway, hallway, and down the steps without a sound.

Once the dark figure arrived at the bottom of the steps it shouted,

"HE'S MINE!"

I awoke with sweat streaming down my face. I jumped from my tangled bedclothes and raced to Ryan's room where I opened the door and peered inside to see my sleeping son.

"Dear God, I'm glad that was only a dream," I prayed.

Chapter 12

Morning finally arrived and I could crawl out of my bed into the wakeful world that was not filled with bad dreams and restless tossing and turning.

It seemed that all three of my offspring were running in slow motion so I had to push hard to get each of them to kick it into gear.

"Let's go, girls, the bus will be here soon," I shouted as I tried to get them to move a bit faster.

"Come on, Ryan, get your backpack. Did you get your lunch money off the table? Move it now. I see the bus down the road at the Simpson house," I said hurriedly.

I didn't have time to talk to Ryan about his phone conversation with his father. I guessed I would have to do it when he came home from school.

Suddenly all the hustle and bustle was gone and I could finish my chores before driving to work and into Wayne's world.

I really wished I liked Wayne more than I did. I really wanted not to grimace with the thought of seeing him and talking to him.

I often wondered how he treated his wife and daughters because he was awful with his employees. Believe me, I have talked to previous employees who worked under Wayne's leadership and each one expressed the same feelings that I did. That was a real shame.

The half hour drive was pleasant and I had my window rolled down about half way so I could feel the fresh clean air blowing all around me.

I pulled into the parking lot and noticed that Everett's car was already parked in the space next to me.

I hurried into the office to discover the reason for Everett's early arrival.

"Everett, you're here early," I said as I walked passed the kitchen area to look out the back door.

"Hey, Lindsay, yeah I am early. I had a few things to do before I go to court," he said cheerfully.

"Do you need me to help in any way?" I asked sincerely. I considered helping Everett a pleasure because he knew how to treat the people who worked with him and that was with respect.

"No, I don't think so. Anna did most of it for me a few days ago. You know, she's learning pretty fast. I'm glad you chose her, Lindsay," he said kindly.

"Me, too, Everett. I think she is a pretty sharp young lady," I agreed.

I returned to my office and looked at the pile of stuff Wayne had placed in the middle of it which included a dictation tape that I immediately popped into place so I could get started.

Soon I heard the front door open and close. It was time for Anna to arrive so I didn't check out front to see who it was.

I chose to use Wayne's intercom system and yelled, "Is that you, Anna?"

"Yes, it's me. I'll be there in a sec," she replied loudly.

I listened to Wayne drone on about a couple of changes I needed to make for the Jones closing. Next, he told me what to do about the Saracin and Edwards closings.

"Lindsay, how are you?" asked Anna as she stood in my doorway.

"I'm fine but you're not. What's wrong?" I asked as I watched her face cloud up as she fought the tears that were trying to slip from her pretty blue eyes.

"Oh, I don't know. I just feel like crying," she said as she put her hands up to cover her face.

"You've got to have a reason, Anna. You just don't cry over nothing," I said as I rose from my chair and walked toward her. I placed my arms around her for the support I thought she needed.

"My dog died. I found her this morning and she was dead. I don't know why she died. She was only about ten years old and was so healthy. There was no reason for her to die," she sobbed.

I wanted to ask her a few questions, but I knew she wouldn't be able to answer them for a few minutes. I led her to one of my client chairs and let her sit until she could try to stop crying.

Everett heard her crying and walked in to see if he could help.

I told him what Anna had told me and he hugged her close. Everett was full of sympathy and compassion but Wayne was not. I hoped that Anna would be okay before Wayne arrived. He would not be sensitive to her feelings like Everett.

I left Anna sitting in my office and went in search of coffee for all three of us.

Everett followed me.

"I think it's strange that her dog suddenly died, Everett," I said in a whisper so Anna wouldn't be able to hear me.

"You think so?" he asked me.

Chapter 13

I thought about the death of Anna's dog and the fact that it occurred so soon after Wayne let it be known that he was representing Steven Armstrong. It was probably a coincidence. I myself once had a dog, a Chihuahua, my beloved Nikki, that died at the age of ten in human years of an obvious stroke. It can happen.

Jumping to a conclusion, right or wrong, was something my mind did quite often. Because I've worked in a law office for so many years, with the attorneys representing all kinds of people from all walks of life, I tend to focus in on the seamy side of life I see so often.

The day was hard and tedious with many added changes to all of the closings but I did get the Jones closing completed and set for action the next day.

Wayne had not indicated that he needed me to stay late. I had completed all the punching of holes and sorting information into his file so he was set for whatever his next step would be as far as the Armstrong file was concerned.

I was looking forward to spending a quiet evening with my kids. Perhaps renting a move and making bowls of popcorn.

I had discovered nothing new on the Armstrong matter. I had nothing to report to Jed and Marnie. I hadn't heard from them during working hours so I thought the matter would remain silent for the day.

As soon as I opened my front door my quiet evening came to an abrupt halt.

"Mom, we've got to do something," pleaded Emily.

"About what?" It was all I could do to force the words out of mouth.

"Mr. Armstrong didn't kill James and Jackie. We know he didn't do that. He is really a nice man who loves his kids very much," added Ellen.

"All right, all right. I believe you. I don't think he killed them but what can I do about it?" I said in a calming tone.

"Something – we've got to do something. The kids at school said he would be put to death if he is found guilty, Mom. That's not fair," said Emily.

"Why do you believe in Mr. Armstrong? What did he do or say that made you believe in him?" I probed trying to understand why they felt so strongly.

"It's the way he held his kids close to him, protecting them, like you hold us, Mom, when we are scared or upset. He truly loves James and Jackie. He would never hurt them," said Ellen.

"The look in his eyes made me believe he was doing the best he could with what he had which wasn't much. You saw his home, Mom," added Emily.

"Okay, yeah, well, if you have that much faith in him, then I will trust your instincts and we will try to help him. Ryan, I want you in on this, too. We will all work together to find James and Jackie," I said as an encouragement to my children trying to get them all to work together for a good reason.

"Aww, Mom, do I have to do this?" asked Ryan.

"Don't you want to help your sisters and me with this adventure?" I asked excitedly.

"No," was the sullen reply.

"Why not?" I asked sharply.

"I don't even know him or the two kids. Why should I care?" he added in a huff.

I had always wanted my children to be honest with me no matter what. Now, I'm not so sure that was a good idea. Sometimes being too honest can be so very hurtful. Even if the hurt was unintended, it could still leave mental marks according to the choice of words that were spoken.

"Because, I do, your sisters do, and he is a neighbor; that's why we all need to watch out for each other and that includes our neighbors," I explained as I fought hard not to raise my voice.

"All right, all right, I'll do what you tell me. Is that what you want?" he asked sullenly.

"Yes, I suppose," I said as the thought about his conversation with his father crossed my mind. Now was not the time to ask; not in front of his sisters.

"What can we do, Mom? How can we help Mr. Armstrong?" asked Emily.

"Jed, Marnie, and I have already started digging around to find out about Mr. Armstrong's past. And yes, we already talked about it and we don't think he killed his kids," I explained to two smiling daughters and a not so happy son.

"Is there anything we can do help?" pleaded Ellen.

"Yes, I think so but you need to do this secretly without letting anyone know why. Do you understand what I am saying?" I asked the three sets of staring eyes.

Heads nodding up and down from the three of them allowed me to continue.

"Talk to your classmates and best buddies to see if they know anything. Maybe ask your teachers if they know him and his children. That's all for now that I want you to do," I said.

"You just want us to snoop around like you do sometimes. Is that it?" said Emily.

"I don't snoop," I said defensively. "I just ask questions, that's all."

"I call that snooping, sticking your nose in where it doesn't belong," said Ryan sullenly.

"In this case, my nose and your noses belong because we are trying to help," I said trying to justify my tactics.

"It's still snooping," add Ryan as he left the room presumably to do his homework.

The long talk with my kids had thrown my evening plans off schedule. I prepared supper, helped with homework, and scooted everyone off to bed.

Chapter 14

This day was going a little smoother than the previous morning when I had trouble pushing my kids out of the door to catch the school bus. The girls were excited about starting their task for helping Steven Armstrong and Ryan seemed a little happier.

Before I could get myself out the door to go to work my telephone rang and Marnie greeted me.

"Hey, Linds, have you found out anything new?" she asked.

"Not a thing. Just the ordinary run of the mill motions that get filed in all criminal court cases," I answered as I looked around the room and decided the straightening could wait until I got home again.

"I found out that Mrs. Darlene Armstrong is the one who has legal custody of the two children. Steven Armstrong stole them and hid them away from her claiming that she was an unfit mother," she said quickly. "I know how you feel about that kind of thing, Linds, so I thought you should know this part right away."

Marnie had heard me gasp when she said the words 'stole' and 'unfit mother.' I had lived through that ordeal myself and I didn't wish it to happen to anyone else.

"Is she unfit?" I whispered.

"I think so; supposedly she is on drugs, prescription drugs," said Marnie.

"That's different," I said with a sigh. "Maybe he did the right thing but who knows? How did you get this information? I hope it wasn't from a file."

"No, just talk, gossip that is. I didn't hear any of it from the people who are working on prosecuting him," she said defensively.

"Good, I don't want you to get into trouble, Marnie," I added.

"I'm not that stupid," she said sarcastically.

"Well, I've got to get out of here and go to work. I'll give you Jed's phone number and you can give him a call, okay?" I said hurriedly as I rattled off his cell phone number.

"Sure, talk to you later," she said and I heard a click when she disconnected the phone line; then, I heard another click, much fainter; but nevertheless, it was a click. Someone had been listening to my conversation.

I ran through the house checking each room where there was a telephone extension but no one was there. I knew there wouldn't be anyone there; the kids went to school already.

I grabbed my handbag and prepared to go to work. After I started the car, I jumped out to check the junction box on the outside of the house where the phone line was connected.

The grass and weeds were mashed down around the area but that could have happened when Ryan was outside playing ball or messing around with his buddies.

I opened the cover and looked inside of the junction box where I saw an odd red clip attached to the line.

Someone was tapping my phone line. Was Justin doing that? Was that the secret he and Ryan were sharing? I wouldn't put it passed him. If he had the capability, I'm sure he would do it; especially if he wanted Ryan to leave me and move in with him.

"No, I'm jumping to conclusions," I said as I scolded myself for thinking bad thoughts about Justin. "Maybe it's related to the Armstrong problem. Maybe whoever it is doesn't want me to find out anything that can be used to defend Armstrong. Maybe I am doing the right thing.

"Oh, God, is this going to be dangerous?" I asked as I threw up my hands towards the heavens.

Chapter 15

Wayne was out most of the day, doing what, I didn't have a clue. Most likely, his absence was due to the Armstrong case. He seemed to be totally immersed into the checking out the background of Steven Armstrong, his family, and his friends. He was trying to look under every rock where those kids could be hiding. From his mood when he entered the office to conduct the Jones closing; things were not going well.

It was evident that he considered the Jones real estate closing as a nuisance, a distraction from more important matters. He rushed through everything pausing briefly between each step to discourage questions that would require lengthy explanations.

Because I had to sit next to Wayne throughout the entire ordeal, I was totally embarrassed by his flagrant 'don't bother me' attitude and his sharp, sarcastic answers to questions posed by the Joneses who were the buyers.

Wayne left the room as soon as all of paperwork was signed and I was left alone to atone for his rudeness.

"Mr. and Mrs. Jones, if you have any questions I will try to answer them. If I can't, I will get an answer from Mr. Maxwell for you. He is now in the middle of investigating a murder case and is quite distracted by the whole ordeal," I explained apologetically.

"When will we get the recorded copies?" asked Mr. Jones.

"I will take them to the courthouse the early part of next week to have them recorded. Then I will mail copies to you," I said in answer.

"It is okay for us to move into the house, isn't it?" asked Mrs. Jones.

"Sure, everything about the financing has been taken care of by the bank. All they need is the deed and deed of trust and I will hand carry it to them. They have already issued the check for me to give to the seller which I am doing now," I said as I handed a check to the Thompsons for payment of the house purchased by the Joneses.

"Is that all we need to do?" asked Mr. Jones.

"Yes, sir," I answered politely with a smile.

"Thank you so much," said both buyers and sellers as they all exited the room.

I walked them to the front door and heaved an enormous sigh.

Anna looked at me and said nothing because words couldn't have expressed how we both felt.

I knew for a fact that all lawyers weren't as abrupt and rude as Wayne. *Why couldn't he be a little bit more like Everett,* I wondered?

I knocked on Wayne's door to gain admittance into his office.

"Do you want me to stay late, Wayne?" I asked praying he would say 'no'.

"No, I don't think so but probably tomorrow because I have to have some motions prepared. Did you set up the other real estate closings yet, the Saracin and the Edwards?"

"No, sir, I need you to let me know what dates you have available? I wasn't sure because of the Armstrong case and the motions that are to be heard," I said.

"You go on home. I will check my calendar and leave you a note. Keep in the mind that the dates could have to be rescheduled at a moments notice. You might want to tell the parties involved about that possibility. Also, I will be working out the office tomorrow talking to Armstrong's friends and family if I can find any," he said in a much milder tone, almost depressed tone.

"Yes, sir," I said as I started to leave his office. "Have a good evening, Wayne."

I meant what I said about wishing Wayne a good evening because I knew if his evening was good, my life in his office would be easier to withstand.

I drove home without the usual scowl on my face. All it took was a few words in a normal tone from Wayne to lift my spirits. Sometimes, he actually treated me like a human. He didn't knock me down with his condescending tone.

My kids were home before me as was always the case but I wasn't worried about them. I knew they would be fine until I got there. After all, the girls were thirteen and had been trained as babysitters so they could be trusted to keep an eye on Ryan.

Everyone was off in his or her bedroom working on school homework when I arrived home. I walked to the kitchen and started preparing supper. Spaghetti, garlic bread, and salad were on the menu for everyone because they all liked that choice of foods.

One by one each of my children became aware of the smells of dinner cooking and followed the scents to the kitchen to ask when we would eat.

By the time I put the salads and bread on the table they were all ready to dig in. I guess they were hungry and I was glad to see that.

We did very little talking while eating but as soon as we ate our last bites, conversations were started.

"Mom, Ellen and I asked all of our friends about the Armstrongs but none if them seemed to know them or anything about then," said a disappointed Emily.

"We talked to as many teachers as we could and none of them knew the Armstrongs. Wouldn't James be old enough to go to school? He is six," said Ellen who also sounded disappointed and confused.

"I would have thought so," I said. "He would be in kindergarten or first grade depending on which side of the school year his birthday occurred."

I wondered if Armstrong had not signed James up for school because he was afraid his ex-wife would find him. I didn't think I should mention that to my kids, not yet anyway. They had had to go through the ordeal of being stolen by their father and I didn't want to remind them again of what it was like.

"Ryan, did you find out anything?" I asked.

"Bobby said that the Armstrongs lived next door to him. He told me that Mr. Armstrong would not let his kids outside to play unless he was standing there watching them. I thought that was kind of stupid because they have a fenced-in yard. All he had to do was lock the gate and they couldn't go anywhere," Ryan said.

"What else did Bobby say?" I asked with interest.

"He said he kept his blinds closed all of the time but he was always peeking through them. You know, spreading them apart so he could see out," answered Bobby.

"Anything else?" I asked Ryan,

"Who was he hiding from, Mom?" asked Ryan.

"I don't know, but we are going to find out," I answered with sincerity.

"Mom, what else can we do?" asked Emily.

"You've done everything you can for now. You've all done a really good job of trying to help. We will figure this out, you know," I said with as much encouragement as I could muster.

My children went to their bedrooms to do whatever kids do at their ages and I was left to work around the house and think about my next step.

Before I finally decided to climb into bed I did a computer search for Steven Armstrong. Nothing came up on the screen about a Steven Armstrong located in Virginia.

I thought that was peculiar because Jed said he had gone to school with Steven Armstrong.

There had been a divorce and custody battle for the kids somewhere in his life timeline. I would have thought something about Steven Armstrong's past would have hit the public records somewhere; especially if he had ever been using the Internet for any reason.

I knew my life could be tracked on that piece of public spyware. Why not his?

I fell asleep and slept soundly, no tossing and turning.

Chapter 16

Wayne was going to be out of the office all day but I still had a lot of work to do.

I hurried my kids along to get them out the door and onto the school bus.

When I climbed into my car I chose to take a different route to work. I drove to the next block and traveled slowly down the street to get a good look at the Armstrong house.

It looked buttoned-up behind blinds that hid the inside from everyone.

I was surprised to see no crime scene tape blocking everyone from looking around the premises.

So – I decided it was a sign that I should check it out myself.

There were definitely no signs of life present inside or outside the house. Again, I accepted that as an open invitation to find the truth.

I parked my car two houses away from the Armstrong abode, climbed out, and walked slowly to the closed gate where I unlatched it and let myself into the yard.

The place had an eerie feeling of foreboding oozing up from the ground. My mind was playing tricks on me again.

"Straighten up, Lindsay," I told myself as I walked up the sidewalk to the front door.

I knocked. It was the polite thing to do just in case someone was lurking on the other side of the door.

Of course, there was no answer to my knock, so I walked to the windows at each side of the door to try to peek inside. The blinds were blocking all prying eyes from seeing the interior.

I checked the door again and noticed a small window up high on the door that I could not reach to see inside. I found a wooden crate under an old flower pot full of dead flowers. I carried the crate to the front door and climbed on top of it, praying that it would hold my weight.

I peeked inside and saw that the living room looked the same as it did when I spoke with Armstrong about my girls babysitting for his kids.

I don't know what I expected to see, but it looked like a normal, lived-in house.

I turned the doorknob and discovered that it was locked.

"Darn," I mumbled as I climbed down off the crate, placed it back where I found it earlier, adorned with the dead flowers.

I walked around the house trying the whole time to look nonchalant. I didn't feel nonchalant. I was actually scared to death.

I reached the back door and was surprised to see a car parked in the backyard. Of course, it was Steven Armstrong's car. He would have put it back there to keep it out of sight if he were hiding like I thought he was.

There was an enclosed back porch so I opened the first door to enter the area of the porch that led to the back door of the house. I reached up from the step-down area to the porch floor and turned the doorknob. The door opened and creaked loudly as it swung inside.

I froze for a moment. I didn't know if I should enter the kitchen, or not.

My curiosity won the battle that was raging in my mind and I slowly entered the room.

The kitchen was clean with no dishes, cups, or anything else in the sink. My own kitchen was rarely that clean.

"How odd," I said as I walked through the room in search of the bedrooms.

The first bedroom must have been Steven Armstrong's because it had a musky, manly smell to it. The bed was made and blue jeans were hanging in the closet along with a couple of button type sports shirts.

The next room must have belonged to the kids but there was no evidence of children ever being in the room. All toys, clothes, signs of children had been removed leaving the twin beds and dressers empty and devoid of ever having been used by James and Jackie.

"What happened to the kids?" I mumbled as I left the lifeless bedroom

I walked to the back door and glanced at my watch. Anna should be at the office by this time. I entered the office number onto my cell phone.

"Wayne Maxwell, Attorney at Law, Anna speaking," she answered cheerfully.

"Anna, this is Lindsay. I'm running a little late. I will be there soon. Do you want me to pick up something?" I said trying not to give a reason for my tardiness.

"Yes, get me an Egg McMuffin. I'm hungry this morning," she answered.

"Okay, see you soon. Oh, by the way, has Wayne called? He said he would be out of the office today but he usually calls in to see if I'm there. You know how he is," I said.

"No, but I'm sure he will. I'll tell him you are picking up something at the courthouse if he does call," Anna said.

"Thanks, Anna. See you soon," I said and disconnected.

Once I was outside of the house I headed directly to the parked car. I tugged at the door on the driver's side but it was locked as was the back door on the same side. I walked around the car looking inside of it through the windows and tugged at the front passenger door. Locked.

I stepped around to the back passenger side door and tugged at it expecting it also to be locked. Much to my surprise the door opened. That happened a lot when there were kids on the premises. They forget to lock doors.

Unlike the bedroom, the car showed signs of children. There was a teddy bear on the floor of the backseat and a small metal toy car next to it.

I slipped my hand and arm between the window and the headrest of the front seat, barely reaching the lock latch to open the driver side door.

I walked around the car after climbing out of the back passenger side, leaving the door unlocked exactly as I had found it to the front driver side and climbed into the car where I sat down on the front seat behind the steering wheel.

I reached up to the sun visor that swung away when not in use. I pulled it down and a small piece of paper fell on me. I snatched it up and saw that written on it was a telephone number. I held onto that piece of paper and then reached over to the glove box. Only car related items were filling the box that included the car registration in the name of Marvin Jenkins and a title signed over to Steven Armstrong from Marvin Jenkins.

"He didn't register the sale with the Department of Motor Vehicles," I mumbled.

I found a small notebook in my handbag and wrote down the important information from the title. I was going to check with Marvin Jenkins to see what he knew.

I kept the piece of paper on which the phone number was written. I was going to definitely call that number. If it was important enough for him to keep it, it was important enough for me to call it. Anyway, I figured that the police had already checked the car and the house. There was no reason to worry about it now.

Chapter 17

I was more than an hour late getting to work, but Anna told me that Wayne had not called to check up on me.

"Thank you, Lord," I whispered as I handed Anna her Egg McMuffin.

"What were you doing?" asked Anna as she pointed at the smudge of dirt I had managed to get onto my sleeve.

I brushed at the dirt and said, "Checking on a house for a neighbor who isn't at home."

"Oh, that's nice. Was everything okay?" she asked curiously.

"Sure, why do you ask?" I said as I looked at her.

"You seem a little disoriented like you have something important on your mind," she said urging me to talk.

"I've got a lot of work to do and I'm getting a late start," I answered vaguely as I walked toward my office.

Under normal circumstances I would have told Anna about the need to prove Armstrong's innocence. This time, I was afraid my curiosity was going to get me into trouble and I didn't want her trying to walk that same tightrope because Wayne was representing Steven Armstrong.

Also, there was the fact that Marnie, who worked for the opposition, was involved; and Jed, a newspaper reporter was the instigator of this whole snooping idea because he went to school with Armstrong.

I had the Saracin and Edwards closings scheduled by noon for the following week.

I stayed in for lunch and asked Anna to pick me up a hamburger when she went out. Of course, I had to answer the telephone and tend to the lobby while she was out getting lunch.

I heard the door open and I rose from my chair to check on who had entered the lobby.

The FedEx man, Harold, was waiting for me.

"Package for Mr. Maxwell," he said cheerfully as always was the demeanor of Harold.

I signed for the package and placed it on Wayne's desk. I was curious about the envelope because it was from a detective agency.

"Did he actually pay to have Armstrong investigated?" I asked myself.

When I returned to my office the telephone rang.

"Wayne Maxwell, Attorney at Law, Lindsay Harris speaking," I said automatically.

"Lindsay, this is Jed," he whispered softly.

"Hi, Jed, what do you need?" I returned with a smile etched across my face.

"I don't always need anything, do I?" he asked.

"Nope. Now—what can I do for you?" I asked with a giggle.

"Have you found out anything?" he whispered softly as if he were hiding the conversation from someone.

"Yes, I have, but I need to ask you a question first," I answered. "What?"

"Is Steven Armstrong his real name?" I asked.

"Why do you ask?" Jed said.

"Just a hunch. I don't think that was his name when you went to school together. If I can find a high school yearbook, I can prove it. What year did you graduate?" I asked.

"You're right. It wasn't Steven Armstrong," he answered.

"What was it?" I asked.

"Sam Jenkins," Jed answered.

"Was he related to Marvin Jenkins?" I asked.

"Yes, how do you know that?" demanded Jed.

"Found a car title with Marvin Jenkins and Steven Armstrong written on it," I explained.

"What else?" Jed asked.

"Nothing much, except that all signs of the children were removed from the house they lived in, but whoever did the removal forgot about the car parked out back. There were toys in the car along with the car title," I said with the idea that I would not tell him about the telephone number, not yet anyway. I wanted to check it out before I let him have it.

"Anything else?" he probed.

"Yes, I think my home phone is bugged," I said as if that were an everyday occurrence.

"Really? Why?" he said.

"Could be a couple of reasons and one is my ex-husband trying to catch me doing something I shouldn't be doing around my kids," I said sharply.

"You didn't do anything bad, Linds. What does he think you're doing?" he sputtered.

"I don't know. He is trying to prove I'm an unfit mother any way that he can so he can take my kids away from me," I said angrily.

"If it isn't him, who else could it be?" he asked.

"Maybe it's related to the Armstrong case. What do you think?" I asked Jed.

"Who knows? Who knows besides Marnie and me that you're working on the Armstrong case?" he asked skeptically.

"Well, my kids do now but the tap was there before I told them what I was doing. I asked them to check with their friends to see if anyone knew the Armstrongs. Ryan's friend, Bobby, lives next door to the Armstrongs so he knew a little about them," I said.

"What was it that Bobby knew?" Jed asked.

"That Mr. Armstrong was secretive and hiding from someone. That's all," I said.

"I'll call you on your cell phone when you're at home. Make sure you leave it on, okay?" he said.

"Sure, no problem," I answered.

"Gotta go," he said abruptly and disconnected the call. That was a sure sign of encroachment by his boss into his personal zone.

When five o'clock rolled around, I was glad Wayne had not decided to come into the office late in the day. I was glad to go home to my children.

Chapter 18

When I arrived home I found no children, the house was empty of noise from televisions or video games.

A sticky note was attached to the front of the television located in the living room.

MOM,
RYAN IS TAKING EMILY & ME TO TALK TO
BOBBY ABOUT THE ARMSTRONGS. WE WILL BE
BACK BY SEVEN FOR SUPPER.
LOVE,
ELLEN

I smiled when I read that note.

"I guess snooping really is contagious," I said as I walked into the kitchen to start supper.

A knock at my front door stopped me from supper preparations.

"Hi, Jed," I said as I opened the front door.

"Lindsay, I want to see your telephone junction box," Jed said without explanation of why he appeared at my front door without a phone call.

"Okay, follow me," I said as I left the door standing open and walked to the side of the house.

He opened the box and looked at the wires.

"You're right. I'm going to disconnect this clip. You go inside and see if you still get a dial tone." he instructed.

I ran around the house only to discover that my front door had closed and I was locked out.

"Just a sec, Jed. I have to find the hidden key," I called to him.

"Why?" he asked.

"My front door must have blown closed," I answered as I felt around the top of the window on the left side of the front doorway.

"Wait a minute, Linds. Don't go inside yet," he said sharply.

"Why not?" I asked.

"What if someone sneaked inside?" he asked worriedly.

"Why would anyone do that?" I asked as a chill rolled down my spine.

"Why would anyone tap your phone?" he asked in response.

"You've got a point. I'll wait. You're taller than I am; you can feel around for the key much easier than I am able to do it," I said as I fought back the fear that was rising up inside me.

Jed reached above the window and located the key. He inserted it slowly into the lock trying not to make a noise of any kind. He turned the key slowly and heard a click as the lock snapped open.

Jed held his arm out in front of me so I wouldn't go barreling into the house.

I took his extended arm as the protective warning it was meant to be and I stayed back behind him letting him lead the way.

He turned the doorknob and gave the door a silent tap pushing it open enough to see inside the living room.

Nobody was there.

"Jed," I whispered. "Your imagination is getting as wild as mine. I think the wind blew it shut."

"Yeah, I hope so," he said as he continued to inspect all of the rooms of the house.

When he returned to the living room he picked up my telephone receiver that was on the end table.

"Still has a dial tone," he said he held it to his ear. "I've disconnected the tap that was done outside, but that doesn't mean whoever did this isn't also using an electronic device to do the same thing. Just don't say anything that can be used against you on the phone. Okay?"

"Like what?" I asked.

"If it's you ex-husband, don't make any assignations with your boyfriend such as overnight stays," he said with a smile.

"Maybe I will do just that so he will show his spots," I said as I felt the temperature of my soul starting to rise.

"If that is who you think is doing this, that might be a good idea so you can catch him at it," agreed Jed.

"What if it is someone else?" I asked as I looked around, for what? I didn't have a clue.

"Just don't talk about the case. Tell Marnie to call you on your cell phone, too. Speaking of Marnie, have you heard from her?" Jed asked.

"No, no I haven't. Have a seat and I'll give her a call," I said as I picked up my cell phone.

"No one can listen in on this?" I asked Jed.

"Sure they can. Anyone can if they have the right equipment. It's a little more complicated than a wire tap. Hopefully, your ex-husband wouldn't have access to that kind of equipment," he said in explanation.

I listened while Marnie's number was being reached by my cell phone service.

"There's no answer, Jed," I said anxiously. "Tomorrow is an early morning workday. Marnie wouldn't go anywhere late at night."

"It's only about six thirty," said Jed.

"I know, but she goes straight home after work. She is just like clockwork. She deviates from her straight home route very rarely and usually that's when she is coming to my house for some reason or another. I'm worried, Jed."

"Where are your kids?" he asked.

"At Bobby's house doing some investigating by quizzing him about living next door to the Armstrongs," I answered.

"Get in my car and we will pick up your kids so they won't find you gone when they return home. Then we will all go to Marnie's. How does that sound, Linds?"

I left all of the lights burning brightly as I ran to Jed's car after making sure the door was locked. Jed replaced the key he used and I grabbed my handbag and keys from inside the house.

"Remember where that key is hidden," I told him, "just in case you ever need to use it."

Chapter 19

I told Jed to drive to the next block and pointed out Bobby's house and the Armstrong house next to it.

We both exited the car and walked to the front porch of Bobby's house where we heard a television, but no kid sounds. If there were four kids in that house, I was sure they would be making some kind of noise.

Jed knocked as I continued to listen for kid sounds. The door opened and Bobby's mother was standing before me.

"Hi, I'm Lindsay Harris; Emily, Ellen, and Ryan's mom. Could you send them out here so I can take the home?" I asked as I tried to look past her into the rest of the room.

"Your friend, Marnie, picked them up at your request. At least, that's what she told me. Your kids knew her and said they wanted to go with her because she is your best friend," explained Mrs. Smith.

"How long ago?" I asked.

"About fifteen minutes, I guess. That was all right, wasn't it?" she asked worriedly.

"Yes, no problem. Marnie and I just got our wires crossed, that's all. Which way did they leave?" I asked as I forced a smile to my face.

"They were headed down the street to make the turn to your house. Is there anything else you need?" she asked.

"No, and thank you. I will follow their path and catch up with them," I answered as I turned to leave.

As soon as I climbed into Jed's car I called Marnie's cell phone. No answer, just the recorded voice mail instruction.

"Jed, I'm getting really worried now. Why would Marnie pick up my kids? How did she know they were at Bobby's? Was someone watching them?"

We drove around the block and searched for Marnie's car. It was not parked on the street within two blocks of my house and it was not parked in my driveway.

"Jed, will you go with me to Marnie's house?" I asked as I fought for control of my overtaxed emotions.

"Sure, which way?" he said as he continued to drive.

Chapter 20

"She lives off Main Street in the older part of town. When you get to Main Street I'll tell you when to turn," I said anxiously.

"Have you ever asked Marnie to pick up your kids?" Jed asked.

"Yes, when I know I'm going to be late from work and they have gone to friends' houses. I don't do it often, but it does happen," I explained frantically.

"So they know to go with her when she shows up at the door in your place," Jed said as he reinforced my words.

"Where did she take them?" I asked as I tried to fight off the panic that was flooding through me.

"I think the question should be, why would she take them?" said Jed.

"I certainly didn't tell her to pick them up; so, who would have told her to do that?" I said as I tried to sort the puzzle pieces in my mind.

"I don't think any of this has to do with your ex-husband. I think it is totally and entirely related to the Armstrong case," said Jed firmly as if he were trying to convince himself that what he was saying was true.

"But we are on the side of the defense. Why would Armstrong or Jenkins want to hurt us?" I asked Jed.

"Maybe it isn't my friend. I don't believe it's Sam who is doing this," said Jed.

"Then, who?" I asked.

"I don't know, but we've got to find out who it is so we can get Marnie and your kids back home safe and sound," he answered.

"Should we go to the police?" I asked as I fought the tears that were forming streaks down my cheeks.

"Not yet. I don't know. What do you think?" he asked, seeming as confused as I was.

"Jed, do you need to call anyone to tell them where you are," I said.

"I will after we check out Marnie's place. Now, I'm on Main Street. Where do I turn?"

I directed him to turn left onto Marion Avenue, to drive between the tall buildings that rose up on each side, and follow the curves and turns until he saw a tall, three story, white clapboard structure straight out of the late eighteen hundreds.

The road was lined with tall trees and street lights that dimly lit the way.

This old, moneyed part of town always frightened me with its hundred year old mansions reaching for the sky and staring at the passerby in a leering, forbidding manner.

"Marnie lives in this part of town?" asked Jed.

"Yes, she comes from old money. You wouldn't know it from talking with her, but she will never be hurting for lack of funds like we are sometimes," I explained.

"Why is she working as a file clerk? Didn't she go to college?" asked an incredulous Jed.

"Yes, she went to college. She wants to be a file clerk. That's what she has chosen to do for now. I think that will change eventually, but I don't know when," I answered.

After maneuvering his car down the long drive to the house, we climbed out and walked to the front porch. It was one of those wrap around porches that extended completely around the enormous house. Not like the modern day decks, this porch was completely roof covered and full of all different types of outdoor furniture. It looked as if the owner was trying to make the foreboding structure look more inviting by sprinkling it with bright patterns of color.

In my opinion, it didn't work. It looked fake and screamed at me to go away which is really what I wanted to do.

Jed knocked and I stood by his side thinking about the few times I visited Marnie's family home or perhaps I should call it the family estate.

Never had I felt comfortable being admitted to her home by a maid or a butler and she had both. I felt as if I were walking into a movie portraying a make believe world that I was not part of but only a viewer.

Marnie never 'put on airs' as my grandmother would say. I was truly shocked when I found out that she was part of the Gillespie family whose roots went back to creation in this part of Virginia. I've never checked out their family tree but I imagined it would be traced to Adam and Eve.

Jed knocked again and the door was opened by an elderly man whom I knew to be the butler, Evan.

"Evan," I said loudly due to the fact that he was hard of hearing, "may I speak with Marnie?"

"Miss Marnie went out earlier this evening and hasn't returned," he stated without any kind of expression other than the professional stone face he was trained to display.

"Do you know when she will return?" I asked.

"No, Madam, she did not say," he said with no emotion.

"Do you know where she was going?" I probed.

"As I recall, she was going to your home, " he answered with a barely noticeable flicker of concern in his eyes.

"Thank you, Evan," I said as I turned to Jed and urged him to walk away with me by pulling at his arm.

"We didn't get anything out of that," said Jed as we walked toward the parked car.

"Yes, we did," I said.

"Like what?" asked Jed.

"Evan is worried about Marnie," I explained.

"Where did you get that idea? The man is made of stone," said Jed as he shook his head in emphasis.

"There was a flicker of worry in his old eyes. I saw the fear and he knows I saw it," I said with a voice ready to break from stress.

"I didn't see it," Jed said.

"I know because he tried to hide it," I said as I opened the car door to climb onto the passenger seat.

"Get in," said Jed.

"No, I don't think so," I said.

"Now, what are you going to do?" he asked.

"I want you to slam your driver side door hard so Evan can hear it. I'm going to pretend to get into the car by slamming the passenger door loudly so Evan can hear that door, too. Then, I'm going to walk to the back of the property where they have other structures where I will check each and every one of them myself. In the meantime, you drive back to the road and out of sight until I call you on my cell phone and you can pick me up, okay?"

"That's a crazy idea, Linds. That could also be a dangerous idea. I'm not going to let you do that alone," he said sternly.

"You have to. Evan has to see the car leave the premises," I said as I tried to convince Jed and myself that this was a good idea.

"Then what? Wait for a phone call? How long?" he demanded.

"It'll take me about a half hour to get a look at all of the buildings. Please call someone in your family and let them know what you are doing for both of our sakes," I pleaded.

"Okay, okay, but I don't like this, Linds. It's too dangerous," he said gruffly.

"It's dangerous only if Marnie and my children are hidden or hiding here. You know that. If you don't hear from me in a half hour, call the police and tell them to come running. This place gives me the creeps on a normal day. Please call someone," I said as I slammed the car door and hid in the trees that lined the driveway.

Chapter 21

I was glad I had chosen black clothing because I blended well into the shadows of the trees under which I was hiding.

My dark blonde hair didn't shine like a beacon but I knew my pale skinned face would light up like the moon in any kind of light.

As much as I didn't want to do it, I knew I had to blacken my skin a bit. I reached down to the area beneath the trees scratching at the fallen leaves and grass until I felt the cold earth. I dug at the dirt until it made both of my hands filthy then I rubbed my hands onto my face. I could feel my skin darkening with the coating of dirt. After applying my disguise to my face, I went to work on the back of both hands trying to hide the whiteness of my skin.

Once I felt a little more camouflaged , I started walking toward the multi-car garage. Actually I was trying to sneak to the garage by stooping over trying to get my size 16 body as low as it would go without forcing me to my hands and knees.

Size 16, by some standards, is obese; but, by my standards, it was comfortable. I have been thinner and I have been fatter; but size 16 seemed to be where my weight thermometer wants to stay.

I was happy with my size because I could still do most everything that a thin person could do and still not kill myself with stupid diets that didn't work.

Anyway, I am almost forty years old, so what if I'm a size 16?

I approached the right side of the garage and scooted along the entire structure looking for a window. There were pockets of complete blackness where I couldn't see a thing. I had to feel my way along that garage because I could not see where I was going.

Finally, I slid up against a window frame but the window was covered by shutters.

I felt my way up the shutters looking for some kind of outside latch. Then my common sense kicked in and I reasoned that the latch was probably on the inside so prying eyes couldn't open it from the outside to look in.

I continued feeling my way to the back of the garage where I found another window and a few unwelcome splinters in both hands. The shutters on this window were not latched because I felt a little movement when I touched one of them.

I stiffened as I backed away from my flat position against the backside of the garage.

I straightened my spine to as tall as my five foot two inches would go and pulled at the shutter closest to me.

This window in the back of the garage was positioned higher from the ground than the one on the side. I had to stretch to my tip-toes to look at the cars parked safely inside for protection from the elements, prying eyes, and possible car thieves.

There was a dim row of lights toward the front of the garage that let me see the cars so I could determine if Marnie's was one of them

It was.

"Evan lied to me," I mumbled as I closed the shutter as softly as I could.

Now that I had checked out the garage, I needed to move on to the next building that I assumed was used for storage of outside tools.

By now the darkness was overwhelming. All I could do was walk toward the darkest points that jutted out against the black sky.

"Marnie is going to have to put some kind of outdoor light back here," I mumbled at about the same time I walked into the pole that was erected in the center of the back yard. I looked up to see the shadows of a light fixture that was broken and swinging from the extended metal arm that had held it.

"Well, maybe Marnie did have a security light," I said softly and apologetically. I knew I should keep my mouth shut and remain silent, but I was scared. Hearing a voice even if it was my own voice seemed to boost my courage up a point or two.

Having located the light pole, I stood and strained my eyes to get my location in the back yard.

A dim strip of light from beneath the garage door showed me the direction from which I had come. I turned away from the garage toward where I thought the out building should be.

I held my hands out in front of me trying to feel my way through the darkness to the building for which I was searching.

I touched it.

I found the building.

I leaned my ear against the door but heard no sounds except the skittering of the tiny feet that fled across my foot. I wanted to scream and jump away but thought better of that idea. I wasn't about to let a tiny, little mouse get the better of me. At least, I hoped it was a mouse.

There were no windows on this building. I decided to move to the next one that was further back on the yard set up against the hillside. It was used as a guest house in days gone by so visitors could come and go as they pleased.

Suddenly I thought of the time. I pulled the cell phone from my pocket and discovered my allotted time was almost gone.

I held my hand over the front of the brightly lit screen trying to shield it from unwanted eyes and I pressed the button next to Jed's name.

"Lindsay, are your ready?" he asked excitedly.

"No, not yet. I have one more building to investigate. Just so you know, Marnie's car is in the garage. I believe she and my kids are here somewhere. Give me fifteen more minutes to check out the last building. It's the old guest house all the way out back. See ya," I said as I disconnected because I didn't want him to argue with me about spending fifteen more minutes back here.

I knew there was a little decorative bridge that crossed a small stream bed that filled with water only after a heavy rain.

I walked slowly toward where I thought the guest house was located. I stubbed my toe on something and I so very much wanted to scream a blasphemous curse, but I held my tongue. Then I realized the bridge was what had caused my pain. I crossed it and knew I should be very close to the little house.

I walked onto the small porch and placed my ear against the door. I could hear noises from inside the structure but I had no idea what those noises were.

I kept my ear pressed to the door. I could hear a scraping noise; then a moan or a grunt, then more scraping.

I tried to turn the doorknob but it wouldn't budge. I rattled the doorknob to stir up whoever or whatever was inside. I ran to the side of the small porch as far away from the door as I could get without leaving the area and waited for the occupant of the guest house to open the door and check on the culprit, meaning me, that had touched the doorknob.

The door did not open, so I leaned my ear against it again. This time I heart grunts and moans as if they were coming from taped mouths.

I went to the nearest window and tried to open it. No luck.

I moved on to the back of the little house and tried another window. It moved a little but I couldn't get enough leverage to force it open.

I went in search of a tree. There were plenty of them around but I had to find one with a low hanging, sturdy branch.

Too much time was passing. I had to call Jed.

"Lindsay?" Jed said softly.

"I found someone or someones in the guest house. I'm looking for a sturdy branch to pry the window open. I don't want to break the window because it will make too much noise," I said in a flurry of words.

"I'm on my way," said Jed.

"No, no, they will see the car," I said.

"Then I'll walk." he growled.

"Okay, okay, I do need your help. I don't know if Marnie is in there, or my kids, or maybe the household staff, but someone is in there," I said as I disconnected.

I finally found a limb that I felt would be strong enough. I broke it off from the tree and headed back toward the window.

I shoved the broken end into the small crack I had forced between the window and the sill and I pushed down forcing the window up and open enough for me to get both hands under it. It was a strain but I pushed it up high enough for a person to crawl inside.

Next problem – I needed something to stand on so I could climb inside and free the occupants.

A chair from the small front porch would do it. I grabbed the one closest to me and propped it against the outside wall. I climbed onto the seat of the chair as I prayed it was tall enough for me to make it into the window and what's more that I would not fall through the seat to the ground. The chair creaked under my weight and one of the legs sunk further into the ground than did the other three, but I managed to get a foot, then a leg over the sill.

This was the time I wished I was skinny. Climbing was much easier for a thin person. "Oh, well, up and over," I mumbled.

I could hear more scraping and scooting noises.

I moved toward the sounds and very nearly tripped over a body that was writhing around awkwardly.

"Hold still," I instructed.

I used my hands to feel up the body to the head where I found the tape. It didn't feel like duct tape so I found an end by touch and gave it a yank. It was adhesive tape like you buy for use in your home so it didn't do as much damage as the duct tape would have.

"Who are you?" asked the untapped mouth.

"Lindsay Harris. Who are you?" I asked as I tried to place the voice.

"Sara Martin. I'm the maid," she said as she fought the tears that were distorting her voice.

"Who else is here?" I asked as I tried to feel around for another body and mouth to untape.

"Miss Marnie, but she has been awful quiet. I think something is wrong with her," said Sara.

I was still working in the dark when I started searching for Marnie. I found her lying silently about four feet away from Sara. I located her mouth and pulled away the tape. The fierce pain caused by the tape must have brought her back to the conscious world to join Sara and me.

"Marnie, are you okay?" I asked when I felt her move.

"Lindsay?" she whispered.

"It's me, Marnie. I found you and Sara, but where are my kids," I asked.

"The house, in the house," Marnie answered.

While I worked at untying both sets of hands and feet, I continued talking.

"Who are they?"

"Drug people, they are from Armstrong's past," Marnie said.

"Why did they take my kids?" I said as I fought back the angry tears that were making their presence known.

"They want you to stop investigating and dragging up Armstrong's past. They want me to supply the prosecutor with some proof that he drowned his kids," she continued.

"He didn't drown his kids. What kind of proof?" I demanded in a loud whisper.

"A witness, they were paying a witness to the drowning," she said with a sob.

"Where are the kids?" I asked.

"They have all of them, yours and Armstrong's. They are all in the house somewhere," she said between sobs.

"How many kidnappers are there?" I asked.

"I don't know," she answered.

"How many did you see?" I asked

"Two men."

"Are you well enough to walk, Marnie?" I asked sympathetically.

"I have to be, don't I?" she answered softly.

"Yeah, I guess you do," I replied.

Chapter 22

I guided both ladies to the window I had crawled through and helped them climb out into Jed's waiting arms.

"Jed, did you bring a flashlight?" I asked when I reached the ground.

"Yes."

"Shine it on Marnie's head for a second. I want to check something out," I instructed.

Jed fumbled with the flashlight and directed it to the back of Marnie's head where I could plainly see blood oozing from a gash that was opened up in her dark hair.

"Marnie, you're bleeding," I said as I reached for her.

"I'll be okay," she said as she waved my hand away. "We need to get the kids - all of the kids."

"Marnie, we need to set a blazing fire so we can call 9-1-1 and get the fire trucks here to put it out. What can we burn?" I asked knowing my friends were going to think I had lost my mind.

"The guest house - burn it. I don't ever want to go in there again." she said bitterly.

"Sounds good to me. Jed, you can help me climb back inside so I can set it on fire. Marnie, you and Sara go stand behind the garage so you will be out of sight. I'll set the fire with Jed's help and call 9-1-1. I'll explain to them that the fire trucks need to be escorted by the police and that everyone should be ready for a gun battle," I said as I concocted the whole idea standing there staring at the house where my children were being held hostage.

"Marnie, did the drug people say why they were after Armstrong?" I asked matter-of-factly. I had to know for my own peace of mind.

"Just that his ex-wife owed them and Armstrong was going to testify against them for dealing drugs. They killed his ex-wife and they were going to kill Steven Armstrong, too," Marnie said softly.

"What makes you think the kids are still alive?" asked Jed.

"I know they are. I'm their mother. I would know if anything happened to them. I would feel it in my heart, Jed."

"We'll get the fire going and that should draw them out of the house. When that happens the police can go in the front while everybody else is out back working on the fire," said Jed.

Jed and I climbed into the guest house where we turned the lights on long enough to locate a box of matches and set fire to the curtains on the front window.

We then opened the back door and ran out of the burning house toward the garage where we joined Marnie and Sara.

I dialed 9-1-1.

Chapter 23

The fire had finally gotten big enough for neighbors to see, so the fire department was getting calls that verified, at least, part of the tale I was spinning.

I could hear the fire sirens in the distance, but I could also hear the distinctive wail of the police cars, too.

"Thank God they believe me," I whispered to those standing near me.

At about that same time I heard the back door of the main house slam and I saw four men running out to see where the fire was located.

I ushered the ladies along the side of the garage away from the commotion and directed them to start running up the driveway to get away from the possible gunplay.

With a rumble, the fire trucks turned onto the driveway as the drivers aimed their vehicles toward the burning fire.

The police cars raced across the front yard getting as close to the front door as possible.

The front door opened and my three children could be seen with Emily holding Jackie in her arms and Ellen holding the hand of James. Ryan was standing directly in front of everyone smiling his goofy, "I did it", smile.

I thought there might have been someone guarding the children when the others went out to investigate the fire, but that didn't happen. The only adult left in the house was Evan and he walked out with the children.

The kids, all five of them, were put into the first police car and driven away from the scene.

The remaining policemen each grabbed a rifle, split into two groups, and started walking around the main house on both sides.

By the time they reached the back yard, they had caught all four of the kidnappers off guard and not a single shot had to be fired.

An ambulance was called for Sara and Marnie so they could be checked out at the emergency room.

Jed and I willingly jumped into Jed's car and drove to the police station where I could be reunited with my wonderful children.

Chapter 24

Jed and I spent the whole night at the police station telling our story.

I made him call the "someone" he had called a couple of times earlier, so he or she wouldn't be so worried. I wasn't sure who his someone was. That was something I would have to find out at a later date.

Thankfully, Jed and I weren't arrested for arson because the detectives questioning us agreed that it was a good diversion and probably the safest way possible for everybody involved.

Marnie suffered a mild concussion and both Evan and Sara were checked over by the medical personnel and declared in good condition.

Social Services would be taking care of James and Jackie until their father was released and that should happen no later than the next day.

Jed and I walked out of the police station with my very tired, very hungry children in tow.

He drove us home and came inside to grab a bologna sandwich before he left for his home.

"I'm sorry about getting you involved in this," said Jed apologetically. "I had no idea there were drug dealers involved."

"It wasn't you fault, Jed. I could have said 'no', but I didn't. Go home and get some rest. I'm going to go in to work later this afternoon so I can tell Wayne how he lost his murder client."

All of us, Ryan, Emily, Ellen, and me, piled into my bed and slept until the telephone rang waking us up.

"Hello," I said sleepily into the phone.

"Lindsay, are you okay?" asked Anna.

"Yeah, sure. I'll be in a little later to tell you what has happened. Is Wayne there?" I asked

"Yep, and he wants the whole story," said Anna.

"Did you give him the envelope from the detective agency?" I asked.

"Yes, but he still wants to talk to you," said Anna.

"I'll be there soon, Anna," I said as I hung up the phone.

I dressed in blue jeans and a sweat shirt. I instructed my children to do the same. We all piled into my car and I drove to Wayne Maxwell's office to tell him the story of why he lost a client.

I truly wanted to know if that detective agency was going to tell Wayne the same story that I was going to tell him. It would be nice to have a little back-up.

Wayne wasn't happy with the turn of events, but the detective agency basically told him the same background information that I had uncovered about Steven Armstrong being Sam Jenkins and that he was a hero, not the murderer that Wayne had to defend before God and everybody.

I took a couple of days off to be home with my little family so we could all heal.

I decided I needed to curb my curiosity for a while because, as proven by my children and my best friends; indeed, SNOOPING CAN BE CONTAGIOUS.

ABOUT THE AUTHOR

Linda Hudson Hoagland of Tazewell, Virginia, graduate of Southwest Virginia Community College, has won acclaim for her novels, short stories, essays, and poems. Many of her works have been published in anthologies such as *Cup of Comfort* and *Christmas Blooms* along with the publication of her eight mystery novels, six nonfiction books and a collection of short stories.

A few of the awards won by Linda Hudson Hoagland are as follows:

2012 – Dream Quest One – First Writing Prize/Summer – I Am Mom

2012 – Alabama Writers Conclave – Honorable Mention/ Traditional Poem – A Dream Trip

2012 – Westmoreland Arts & Heritage Festival – Honorable Mention – Short Story – Welcome to Whistler

2012 – Virginia Writers Club Spring Shorts – Second Place – Nonfiction – No Service

2012 – West Virginia Writers Inc – Honorable Mention – Stage Play – I'm Not Ready

2012 – The Seacoast Writers Association – Third Place – Nonfiction – Getting Myself Primed

2012 – Tennessee Mountain Writers Inc – Second Place – Fiction – And the Next Day

2011 – Women's Memoirs – All Things Labor – Honorable Mention - Penance

2011 – Alabama Writers Conclave – Honorable Mention – First Chapter of a Novel – Writing the Circuit/So It Was A Lie (Crooked Road Stalker)

2011 – Alabama Writers Conclave – Second Prize – Juvenile Fiction – The Lady in the Sun

2011 – Appalachian Heritage Writers Symposium – Second Place – Adult Essay – Surprise Package

2011 – Writers-Editors Network International Writing Competition – Honorable Mention – Nonfiction – Getting Myself Primed

2011 – Tennessee Mountain Writers – Third Place – Writing for Young People – I Dare You

2010 – The Jesse Stuart Prize for Young Adult Writing – Second Place – How's That For Real

2010 – Tampa Writers Alliance – Novel – Honorable Mention – Quilt Pieces

2010 – Alabama Writers Conclave – Nonfiction – Third Prize – Four Large Eggs

2008 – Nominee Governor's Award for the Arts

2007 – Sherwood Anderson Short Story Contest – First Place – Category V

Many other awards have not been listed.

OTHER BOOKS WRITTEN BY LINDA HUDSON HOAGLAND:

FICTION

CROOKED ROAD STALKER

THE BEST DARN SECRET

SNOOPING CAN BE DANGEROUS

A COLLECTION OF WINNERS

CHECKING ON THE HOUSE

DEATH BY COMPUTER

THE BACKWARDS HOUSE

AN AWFULLY LONELY PLACE

NONFICTION

90 YEARS AND STILL GOING STRONG

QUILTED MEMORIES

LIVING LIFE FOR OTHERS

JUST A COUNTRY BOY: DON DUNFORD (Edited)

WATCH OUT FOR EDDY

THE LITTLE OLD LADY NEXT DOOR